My Grandmother Carries A Machete

LIANA BROOKS

OTHER WORKS

HEROES AND VILLAINS

Even Villains Fall In Love
Even Villains Go To The Movies
Even Villains Have Interns
Even Villains Play The Hero (books 1 – 3 omnibus)
The Polar Terror

TIME AND SHADOWS MYSTERIES

The Day Before
Convergence Point
Decoherence

FLEET OF MALIK

Bodies In Motion
Change of Momentum
For Every Action (forthcoming)

SHORTER WORKS

All I Want For Christmas Is A Werewolf
Darkness & Good
Fey Lights
Prime Sensations

Find other works by the author at
www.lianabrooks.com

My Grandmother Carries A Machete

INKLET #28

LIANA BROOKS

Inkprint PRESS
www.inkprintpress.com

Print ISBN: 978-1-925825-27-5
eBook ISBN: 9781393350712

www.inkprintpress.com

National Library of Australia Cataloguing-in-Publication Data
Brooks, Liana 1982 –
My Grandmother Carries A Machete
32 p.
ISBN: 978-1-925825-27-5
Inkprint Press, Canberra, Australia
1. Fiction—Coming Of Age 2. Fiction—Short Stories

First Print Edition: February 2020
Cover photo via Unsplash
Cover design © Inkprint Press
Interior art © Amy Laurens

MY GRANDMOTHER CARRIES A MACHETE

MY GRANDMOTHER CARRIES A MACHete.

Really, it isn't anything cool or exciting. She doesn't fight crime or monsters. It's just a gardening tool. And once you see the garden, you realize what she really needs is napalm.

The garden of terror that requires a machete to hack your way to the center started life as a discreet herb garden on the side of the house. It's older than my grandmother, planted by some pioneering ancestor with more enthusiasm than gardening skill.

Planted by someone who didn't realize that those small plants in tidy rows would grow so that the rosemary now resembles a short tree and the parsley is dense enough that small tribes of toddlers have been lost in there.

Perhaps the planter thought the Texas heat would be enough to keep the garden from taking on a life of its own.

Certainly it's a theory that works for the rest of Texas. The easiest way to kill a plant is leave it outside during the month of August and wait for the plant to shoot itself in despair. Even cacti wither and die under the unrelenting heat of the Texas sun.

But not in grandma's garden.

You can ignore the garden, walk away for months at a time, leave it unwatered for years, drop weed killer on it, curse it, exorcise it, even burn incense over it—and yet the garden grows.

My great-grandmother tried giving the plants away. She uprooted the mint and gave it away to everyone who made eye contact. During the worst of Texas droughts you can tell who has the monster mint.

The media dubbed it the 'Glenwood Mint'. The scientists at Texas A&M are still studying rogue clippings, trying to determine how a plant can live with four-inch roots and no water for two years.

That's why Grandma needs the machete.

Every spring, around about March, she pulls the polished weapon from the cupboard over the washing machine, dons her gardening gloves and sandals, and marches into the backyard to see what damage has been done.

This year is different.

She sits in her rocking chair on March second, a tear in her eye as she watches the snapdragons bloom along the front walk. "I can't do it this year," she whispers. She raises a papery hand, sets it on my knee. "Jenny. Go get the machete. It's your turn."

This is it. With a sense of impending doom, I walk into the mudroom. I pull on the gloves and the sandals. I pull the machete from its case, put my cell phone in my pocket in case I need to call for back up, march into the living room and out the back door.

"Grandma! There are tomatoes!"

Grandma moves with blazing speed to peer over my shoulder. "Good googlymoogly," she breathes. "I forgot about them."

"We haven't planted tomatoes in two years!" I choke back fear. Four lush plants beckon, their red fruit tempting the sinner like apples of Eden.

"Get the pots!"

There are four burners on the stove, each large enough to hold a twenty-two gallon stockpot. We have two slow cookers, and each can hold sixteen gallons.

I plunder the tomato orchard. The abandoned plants have grown well over six feet tall; they droop with heavy fruit and spring upright as I pull the tomatoes away.

Stuffing the tomatoes into pots and piling the excess on the long kitchen counter, my grandmother pours water over each set and turns on the heat. "Get garlic," she orders. "You'll find it behind the roses."

I shudder, grab the machete, and stalk into the herb garden of terror.

The rosemary bush towers over me, a fragrant giant. Thick stalks of parsley reach to my knees. But all I can smell is the mint.

In the far corner, I see the rambling

roses that cascade over the front fence in a shower of red and pale pink. Beneath those roses, the fresh garlic grows. I heft the machete in my hand. With grim determination I set out, hacking, slashing, pruning with fervor that is nigh on religious.

I bring the slaughter to Grandma: rosemary twigs as long as my arm, bunches of parsley, enough oregano to stuff a piñata, garlic, wild onions that I found tucked in a corner next to the lavender.

"Tell your cousins to bring garlic bread," Grandma instructs as she stirs the six pots, tasting, testing, and adjusting the flavors until they are perfect. "And call the in-laws, we need extra noodles!"

I go back to the garden to trim yellowed leaves that have never seen sunlight. I slip on fresh loam; my cell phone flies. I scream as my cell phone slips between the thorny canes of the roses, another casualty of the garden of terror. But from my prone position I see a miracle: basil!

"Grandma! Basil!" I hold the aromatic leaves up for her distant perusal.

"The mint must have insulated it from the snow this winter."

I labor my way back to her, bearing my bounty. She rubs the leaves between her fingers, releasing the scent like a lover's perfume. "Perfect."

The next day, as rosy-fingered dawn reaches out to her fleeing love, I roll out of bed and reach for the machete. My machete. I have a cell phone to save and a legacy to keep. The garden must be tamed.

"Holler if you find a body!" Grandma calls.

I walk out the door.

I carry a machete.

THE MAKING OF *MY GRANDMOTHER CARRIES A MACHETE*

This is a very old short story written back when I lived in Texas. It was my first experience gardening in the south and I wasn't entirely prepared for what happened. The mint ran wild. The snapdragons never faded.

And on New Year's Day, in the middle of winter, I found red, ripe tomatoes growing against a south-facing brick wall. The sunshine and shelter of the house had protected the rugged little plants even though I hadn't watered the garden in months.

There was really no choice by to make spaghetti sauce. It was the right thing to do.

The garden is probably gone now. The house long sold to another family. But the memory of the garden lives on.

DOWNLOAD YOUR FREE EBOOK

When you buy a print book from Inkprint Press, we like to say THANK YOU by offering you the ebook for free!

Please head to www.inkprintpress.com/inklets/28/ and the use the coupon INKLET28 to get your copy of this Inklet in epub AND mobi today!
(Coupon will only work once.)

Read more by Liana Brooks!

THE POLAR TERROR

CHAPTER ONE

KADDY LEANED HER HEAD against the pale yellow wall of the hospital room, closed her eyes, and tried not to hear the constant whooshing and beeping of the machines.

The ticky-tick-tick of the heartrate monitor.

The two-minute beep as the IV dropped another controlled dose of pain medications that seemed to do no good.

The whock-whock-whock of the second hand on the clock.

There was no escape.

She couldn't even run outside to the snow and let that peace envelope her. Not while Everett was lying in bed, staring out the window at the flat roof of the parking garage, refusing to talk.

With a sigh, she tried to reach him. Again. "Do you want to watch some TV?"

Everett didn't move.

"We could play with your action figures." She pushed herself out of the uncomfortable chair and walked over to his bed.

Everett let her pull the plush Polar Terror doll out of his listless hand.

She bopped him on the nose with it. "The Polar Terror is coming! He'll walk right out of this storm and—"

Everett rolled to the side, crossing his tiny arms as best he could. His bottom lip quavered with anger and pain.

"I'm sorry." Kaddy put the doll back next to him. "We're going to find a way through this, Ev. I promise. And then we'll sew you the Polar Terror costume you wanted."

"There is no Polar Terror," Everett whispered, his first words all day. "Nobody comes to rescue you."

She rubbed his shoulder gently. "I know, bud. That's why you have me. You and me, we can handle anything."

"Not this," he whispered. "Not cancer."

Tears choked her. "We will," she whispered just as a softly. "We'll find a way to make it all right."

Everett squeezed his eyes shut.

Kaddy slumped back. Even if—and it was a really big if—the hospital pulled off a miracle and Everett got better, she wasn't going back to a job.

Her firm had been very patient, let her take a leave of absence, but her boss was retiring and the incoming boss hadn't liked her.

He'd questioned her education, her field time, her work ethic…

And while the guy couldn't come out and say it, his tone all but screamed SINGLE MOMS NEED NOT APPLY.

She shook her head. Being a single mom hadn't been her choice. She wasn't even dating when Everett was born.

But then there'd been a car accident a semester before graduation. Her sister and brother-in-law were killed on impact.

The idea of being a working, single parent was terrifying, but letting Everett bounce between foster families wasn't an option either.

Squeezing the guard rail of his hospital bed, she stood up. One way or another, she'd make a good life for him. That's what moms did.

There was a tentative knock at the door, like the person on the other side was hoping they wouldn't get an answer, but knew they would.

Rolling her eyes, Kaddy cracked it open for the inevitable nurse.

Andrea, the ever-perky Dream Coordinator for Merriton Pediatric Hospital, looked at her with the world's fakest smile, wide, frightened blue eyes, and damp blonde hair that looked like she'd gone outside without her usual hat.

"Yessssss?" Kaddy dragged the word out.

Andrea squeezed through the tiny crack in the doorway and slammed the door shut. "Okay. Hi, Kaddy! Everett! It is so good to see you two!" The words were rushed, panicked, and had the forced joviality of true terror.

But this was the Yukon in mid-winter, not some American city where a bomber was going to hold them hostage. "Is... is everything okay?" Kaddy asked.

The only thing that would scare Andrea was a really bad diagnosis. Kaddy's stomach flipped as tears welled. She couldn't handle that.

"Just dandy!" Andrea's voice squeaked. "Actually." She faked a laugh. "Funny story. Everett has a visitor. And, I know he's been so tuckered out, the poor thing, so I was thinking we should reschedule. Don't you? That's great!" she rushed on, not letting Kaddy answer. "I'll cancel. He can come back some other time."

Not bad news then.

Everett rolled over in his bed, forehead wrinkled in confusion.

"Who came?" Kaddy asked. The hospital attracted an eclectic group of visitors. Usually hockey stars, medical students, and politicians on goodwill tours. But Andrea welcomed them all with open arms. "It isn't the Maple Leafs again, is it?" No one this far north loved the Maple Leafs.

Andrea's head shook so hard Kaddy worried the woman was going to give herself a concussion.

"Okay…"

Kaddy glanced over at Everett who was showing the first interest in anything since his chemo treatment two days earlier. "Is there a reason you don't want this person to see Everett?" She licked her lips and mouthed, *Is it child services?*

"Worse," Andrea whispered hoarsely. She leaned forward and murmured a name in Kaddy's ear.

Kaddy's eyebrows went up in surprise. "Like... for real? You—" She stopped herself just in time and leaned forward. "You found a cosplayer to play the Polar Terror?"

She couldn't keep the excitement out of her whisper. Everett was going to be over the moon.

"No." Andrea shook her head and glanced over her shoulder. The color drained from her face. "He's... he's not fake."

"Who isn't fake?" Everett demanded from the bed.

"Just say no." Andrea grabbed Kaddy's elbow. "Please?"

Kaddy shook the other woman off and looked at the door.

There was a thin layer of frost on the door. A suspiciously thin layer. Like someone was intentionally cooling the door for a grand entrance.

She narrowed her eyes. Would the Dream Coordinator come in here acting terrified just to sell the idea of a super villain at the hospital? Yes. Yes she would. It was *exactly* the sort of thing a perky, cheerful-before-coffee, former cheer-leader would do.

Kaddy crossed her arms and sighed dramatically. "I don't know, Andrea. Ev's had a really rough week. I don't think he should have visitors. Not even the Polar Terror."

The heartrate monitor screamed in excitement as Everett sat up like he was attached to a spring. "The Polar Terror?"

With a burst of cold air, the door fell inward. Ice crystals glittered as icicles formed on the ceiling.

That was some impressive special effects budget.

A man in the Polar Terror's costume stepped in, towering over even Kaddy, who hadn't been called short since she turned thirteen and shot up. The muskrat parka, a rabbit fur hat, a strip of seal skin, a fur pouch, beadwork on his boots... and of course the very modern black balaclava with the Under Armor logo.

The Polar Terror had come to Merriton.

Keep reading! Head to lianabrooks.com/polar-terror/ to buy your copy now!

ABOUT THE AUTHOR

LIANA BROOKS lives in North America where she enjoys picking wild berries, gardening, and cooking up delicious meals for her family. The door is always open to guests. Dinner is at six. Don't mind the snapdragons guarding the front door, they hardly ever bite.

Brooks is known for her space operas, including the *Fleet of Malik,* a series of connected sci-fi romances about re-building after a decades long war; and the enemies-to-lovers super-hero series, *Heroes and Villains.*

You can find out more about Liana at her website, www.lianabrooks.com.

INKLETS

Collect them all! Released on the 1st and 15th
of each month.

When War
Came to Town
A Powers Story
AMY LAURENS

INKLET #040
NOT QUITE
Cinderella
LIANA BROOKS

INKLET #041
ONE BAD MAN
AMY LAURENS

DOUBLE ISSUE
INKLET #042
The Claustrophobia
Of Loneliness &
Adam, Be A Star
AMY LAURENS

INKLET #043
The Artist
as a Young Girl
LIANA BROOKS

INKLET #044
CONFESSIONS
AMY LAURENS

INKLET #045
But For Snow
A Kaltfass Story
AMY LAURENS

INKLET #046
The Boy
Named NO
LIANA BROOKS

INKLET #047
Anamata
AMY LAURENS

INKLET #048
A Wolf for
Christmas
AMY LAURENS

9 781925 825275